GURPURAB

Om KIDZ
An imprint of Om Books International

Gurpurab, or the 'festival of the gurus', honours the birth of the first Sikh Guru, Guru Nanak.

Also known as Guru Nanak Gurpurab, and Guru Nanak Jayanti, it is one of the most sacred festivals within the religion of Sikhism.

In India, the festival is celebrated with great joy and fervour especially in Punjab, Haryana and Chandigarh, which have a large number of Sikhs.

Guru Nanak founded Sikhism. He was born on the 15th of April, 1469. His birthday is celebrated on Kartik Poornima, which is a full-moon day in the Indian calendar.

This day is celebrated as a national holiday in India. Two days prior to his birthday, a 48 hour reading session of the holy book of the Sikhs, the Guru Granth Sahib is held in gurdwaras, the place of worship for Sikhs.

This reading session is called Akhand Path and continues for two days. To mark the occasion, gurdwaras are decorated with flowers and lights.

The next morning, a procession, known as Nagarkirtan, led by five senior members of the community, is organised. These five members are called Panj Pyare.

The Panj Pyare lead the procession and carry the Sikh flag, called the Nishan and the Palki (palanquin) of Guru Granth Sahib.

Brass bands play various tunes and Gatka teams display their skills with the sword and engage in mock battles using traditional weapons.

On the day of Gurpurab, the celebrations begin early. Hymns from Sikh scriptures are recited in the morning.

This is followed by religious talks or Katha and hymns from the Sikh scriptures called Kirtan, which praise the Guru.

After the Kirtan, Kadah Prasad, a sweet dish made from wheat flour, is distributed to everyone.

After the distribution of Kadah Prasad, community lunch, known as the Langar is served at the gurdwaras. Everyone, regardless of caste, creed or class, is served food.

Some gurdwaras also host night-prayer sessions, which begin at sunset.

Evening prayers called Rehras are recited followed by a late night Kirtan. Gurbani is sung at approximately 1:20 a.m., which is when Guru Nanak was born.

The celebrations of Guru Nanak Gurpurab come to an end in the morning, at around 2 am.